STEPHEN CURRY
I HAVE A
SUPERPOWER

ILLUSTRATED BY
GENEVA BOWERS

Unanimous
Publishing

PENGUIN WORKSHOP

Good evening, folks. And welcome back!

The game is tied 92–92. With four seconds left on the
clock, the home team has possession of the ball ... but who
will they give the ball to for the final shot? Let's watch ...

Meet Hughes. He loves science, his dogs, and the game of basketball. Though he's only eight years old and might seem like your ordinary kid . . . he is anything but ordinary.

Yes. Because, you know, you have a . . .

You know, the thing that makes you extraordinary. A . . . super—

Today is no ordinary day for Hughes.

THANKS! RIGHT! TODAY IS A SUPER. MEGA. HUGE. DAY. BECAUSE TODAY IS THE DAY I SHARE MY SUPERPOWER . . . WITH THE WORLD!

There are only a few people in the whole world who know about Hughes's superpower.

MY COACH, MY PARENTS, AND, OF COURSE, ME!

Now tell them your other secret . . .
it's my favorite part.

Now, I know what you're thinking: "There's NO WAY this short, scrawny kid has a superpower. And there's no way *I* have a superpower."

You got this. Now get out there and show them all your superpower.

I . . . I GUESS I'M WORRIED I STILL WON'T BE GOOD ENOUGH TO KEEP UP WITH THEM.

OK, HERE WE GO . . .

CAN I GET ON A TEAM?

And so began the moment Hughes dreaded: the picking of teams. Aliyah and Kaeden are the two tallest kids in school. They could practically dunk since they were in the second grade.

Desmond and Owen are the two fastest kids out on the court.

Mila and James have sneakers that are guaranteed to make you jump higher.

But Hughes didn't have any of those superpowers. And the one he has isn't something he was born with or learned in a day. No, it was quite the opposite. For months, he practiced every day before and after school.

He **DRIBBLED** his basketball wherever he went.

He **SHOT** free throws every weekend in his driveway.

And he **WATCHED** all his favorite players on television to learn how they played.

With **HEART**, Hughes knows he can overcome any obstacle that gets in his way, because he is prepared and determined. And his **HEART** allows Hughes to never give up on himself.

And remember, folks, having **HEART** isn't just for sports. If you have **HEART** with whatever you're passionate about, you're destined for success. So, until next time, say it with us . . .

To all the kids who feel underrated . . .
you have a superpower, too—SC

To all of those out there ready to embrace
their own superpower—GB

PENGUIN WORKSHOP
An imprint of Penguin Random House LLC, New York

First published in the United States of America by Penguin Workshop,
an imprint of Penguin Random House LLC, New York, 2022

Text copyright © 2022 by Unanimous Media Holdings, LLC
Illustrations copyright © 2022 by Geneva Bowers
Creative Direction by Erick Peyton
Content Editor Kalyna Maria Kutny
Design by Lynn Portnoff

Visit us online at penguinrandomhouse.com.

Library of Congress Cataloging-in-Publication Data is available.

Printed in the United States of America

ISBN 9780593386040   10 9 8 7 6 5 4 3 2 1 WOR